GREAT ILLUSTRATED CLASSICS

HEIDI

Johanna Spyri

adapted by
Deidre S. Laiken

Illustrations by
Pablo Marcos Studio

BARONET BOOKS, New York, New York

GREAT ILLUSTRATED CLASSICS

edited by
Malvina G. Vogel

CONTENTS

About the Author

Johanna Spyri was born in 1829 in the Swiss village of Hirzel. Her house overlooked the mountains, and they inspired her to write the story of *Heidi*.

Johanna Spyri moved to the city of Zurich after she married an attorney. Her yearning for her childhood home in the small village came out in the many children's stories she wrote.

Although the author died in 1901, *Heidi* lives on as a story about the joy of life in the Swiss Alps.

A Footpath Winds up the Mountain.

Chapter 1
The Journey up the Mountain

The Swiss town of Mayenfeld lies at the foot of a mountain range whose rugged peaks tower high above the valley below. Behind the town a footpath winds gently up the mountain.

One sunny June morning, a tall, strong woman was climbing up the path. She had a bundle in one hand and held a little girl about five years old by the other hand. The child's cheeks were flushed and sunburned, and she was wearing two dresses, one on top of the other. She looked like a shapeless bundle of clothing trudging uphill on a pair of shoes.

After climbing for almost an hour, they reached a little village called Dorfli. This was where the woman used to live, and the people of the town remembered her and called to her from their houses. She did not answer, but continued on her way until she reached a house at the very end of the main street. There a voice from inside called to her:

"Half a minute, Detie, and I'll come with you if you're going any farther."

Detie stood still, but the little girl sat down on the ground.

"Tired, Heidi?" Detie asked her.

"No, but I'm very hot," the child answered.

"We'll be there soon. Just keep going, and we'll be there in an hour."

At that moment a plump, pleasant-faced woman came out of the house and joined them. The little girl got up and followed as

Climbing Up the Path

the two grown-ups went ahead, gossiping about people who lived in Dorfli or around it.

The woman finally asked Detie where she was going with Heidi. Detie explained that when her sister died a few years ago, Heidi was all alone in the world. So Detie had taken her in and raised her. But now she had been offered a wonderful job in a good family, but the family lived in a city far away.

"Well then, who will take care of poor Heidi now?" asked the woman.

"I am taking her up to Uncle Alp who lives on the mountain. It's high time he took some responsibility for her. After all, he is her grandfather."

The woman looked shocked. Everyone knew that Uncle Alp was strange. He lived all alone on a mountain. He never talked to anyone in the village, and he hadn't set foot in church for years. He had a wild look in his eyes, and he wore a long white beard. No one

Detie's Friend Joins Her.

really knew how he got the name "Uncle Alp" or why he had lived alone for so many years.

But Detie's friend felt sure that Detie knew more about the old man than anyone else. After coaxing her friend for a little while, the woman got Detie to tell her this story:

"Uncle Alp grew up in a fine house in a lovely village. He was the oldest son and had only one younger brother. Instead of living a quiet life in the village, Uncle Alp longed for the exciting life in the city. He traveled all over, got into bad company, and drank and gambled away all his property. His poor parents died of shame and grief when they heard of it. His brother was ruined too. He ran away somewhere, and no one heard of him again.

"Uncle Alp disappeared too. He had nothing left but a bad name. He was finally discovered in the army in a country far away.

Uncle Alp's Fine House

Then no one heard of him for twelve or fifteen years. One day he reappeared in the village with a young son and asked some of his relatives to look after the boy, but everyone refused. No one wanted anything to do with him or the boy. He was so angry that he vowed he would never set foot in the village again. So he came to Dorfli and settled down there with the boy, whose name was Tobias. No one ever knew what had happened to his wife. Most people believed that she died.

"Anyway, he saved a little money and apprenticed his son to a carpenter. Everyone learned to like the boy, but no one trusted the old man! There were all sorts of rumors about him deserting the army to avoid some trouble he had gotten into.

"All the same, he was accepted as a member of the family. His grandmother and my grandmother were sisters, so we called him Uncle, and since we're related to almost

Uncle Alp Reappeared with a Young Boy.

everyone in Dorfli, the whole village soon called him Uncle too. Then when he went to live on the mountain it became Uncle Alp!

"Anyway, after Tobias learned his trade, he came home to Dorfli and married my sister. They settled down very happily together. But only two years later, he was killed by a falling beam while he was building a house. My poor sister went into such a shock that she fell ill with a fever and never walked again. She only lived for a few more weeks. Everyone said the tragedy was Uncle's punishment for his own mistakes. They told him to his face that he was to blame, and even the pastor told him to do penance to clear his conscience. That made him so angry that he refused to speak to anyone. He went up on the mountain to live and hasn't been down since. My mother and I took my sister's child, Heidi, to live with us. But now I must go away, and there is no one but Uncle Alp to

Uncle Alp Refused to Speak.

take care of her."

Detie's friend looked at her with disapproval. She even told Detie that she was surprised that Detie could hand Heidi over to the old man just like that. But Detie said that she had no choice and continued on her way up the mountain.

Continuing up the Mountain

Peter the Goatherd

Chapter 2
Peter the Goatherd

While Detie was telling her friend all about Uncle Alp, Heidi had become friends with a young boy named Peter. Peter was eleven, and every morning he went down to Dorfli to gather the goats and drive them up to graze in the mountain meadows. Then, in the evening, he brought them down again.

The summer was the only time when Peter could see other boys and girls. For the rest of the time, goats were his only companions. He spent very little time at home with his mother and his old, blind grandmother who lived with them. He left the hut very early and always stayed as long as possible with the children in Dorfli. His father had been the goatherd before him, but he had been killed several years ago while chopping down a tall tree. His mother's name was Bridget, but everyone just called her "the goatherd's mother." Everyone called his grandmother "Grannie."

Now Heidi and Peter were running and playing in the fresh grass on the side of the mountain. Heidi had removed some of her heavy clothing, and when Detie caught up with the two children she scolded Heidi and made her wrap the discarded clothing in a bundle. Peter followed along and carried the bundle for Heidi.

When they finally reached the top of the mountain, there was Uncle Alp, sitting peacefully with his pipe in his mouth and his hands on his knees. Peter and Heidi had run

Running in the Fresh Grass

ahead of Detie. Heidi was the first to reach the old man. She went straight up to him and held out her hand.

"Hello, Grandfather," she said.

"Hey, what's that?" he exclaimed gruffly as he took her hand. She stared at the old man. She was fascinated by his long beard and bushy grey eyebrows. Meanwhile, Detie came towards them while Peter stood and watched to see what would happen.

"Good morning, Uncle," said Detie. "I have brought you Tobias' daughter. I don't suppose you recognize her, since you haven't seen her since she was a year old."

"Why have you brought her here?" he demanded roughly. "And you be off with your goats," he said to Peter. The old man gave him such a look that Peter disappeared at once.

Detie explained to her uncle that Heidi was his responsibility now. She reminded

"Hello, Grandfather."

him that he was the child's closest relative and that he would have to answer for it if any harm came to her.

Uncle Alp got angry at Detie's warning.

"Go back where you came from and don't come here again," he said angrily, raising his arm.

Detie didn't wait to be told twice. She said good-bye to Heidi and ran down the mountain, not stopping till she reached Dorfli.

Detie Runs down the Mountain.

The Old Man Stares at the Ground.

Chapter 3
At Grandfather's

As soon as Detie left, the old man went inside and sat down again. He stared at the ground in silence, blowing great clouds of smoke from his pipe, while Heidi explored her new home.

After she had looked around for a while, she asked the old man to show her what was inside the hut. She picked up her bundle of clothes to take with her. The inside was one large room. There was a table and a chair and a bed in one corner. Opposite that was a stove. There was a door in one wall which the old man opened, and she saw it was a large closet.

"Where will I sleep, Grandfather" asked Heidi.

"Wherever you like," he answered.

This answer pleased Heidi, and she soon discovered a ladder which led to a hayloft. Heidi loved the sweet-smelling hay and decided to make her bed right there in the loft. Grandfather smiled when he saw Heidi so happy. He brought her a pillow, sheets, a warm blanket, and a thick cloth which they used to make a mattress. Heidi was so pleased with her new bed that she could hardly wait to go to sleep. But her grandfather reminded her that she still had not eaten her dinner. So he went to the big stove and prepared a simple but hearty meal for both of them. When Grandfather was finished cooking, Heidi went to the closet and found plates and silverware on a shelf. She set the table,

The Ladder to the Hayloft

and her grandfather smiled and praised her for being so helpful.

Not long after finishing her meal, Heidi became sleepy, for she had had an exciting day. She said good night to her grandfather and climbed into her bed in the hayloft.

During the night the wind blew so hard that it shook the whole hut and made its beams creak. It shrieked down the chimney and brought one or two of the old fir tree branches crashing down. The old man became worried. He thought that Heidi would be frightened. He climbed up the ladder and went to her bed. The moonlight shone through a small opening in the roof, and he could see Heidi's face. She was fast asleep under the heavy blanket. Her cheek was resting on her chubby little arm, and she had a wonderful, happy expression on her face. The old man stood looking at her until the clouds covered the moon and darkened the room.

The Moon Shines on Heidi's Face.

Happy in Her New Life

Chapter 4
A Visit to Grannie

All through that summer Heidi went up to the pasture every day with her friend Peter and his goats. She grew tanned and happy in her new life. She loved her old grandfather, and life on the mountain made her feel as free as the birds that sang in the big fir trees near the hut. But when autumn came, strong winds began to blow and Grandfather said:

"Today you must stay at home. A little girl like you might get blown over the side of the mountain by a gust of wind."

Peter was disappointed when Heidi could

not go with him. He had grown used to her company, and he found it lonely and dull to be without her. The goats were twice as troublesome when she was not there. They seemed to miss her and scattered all over the place, as though they were looking for her.

But Heidi managed to be happy wherever she was. She enjoyed staying at the hut and watching her grandfather at his carpentry and his other jobs.

Then all at once it turned really cold, and Peter arrived in the mornings blowing on his hands to warm them. One night it started to snow. It, snowed until there was not a single leaf to be seen. Heidi watched from the window. She loved the thick white snow and hoped it would go on falling until the hut was buried up to the window sills, so it would be impossible to go out. But that did not happen, and the next morning Grandfather was able to dig his way out and clear a path to

Heidi Watches Grandfather.

the hut. No sooner was the path clear, than Peter came for a visit. He came in and sat by the fire while Grandfather asked him about school.

In the winter Peter went to school to learn to read and write. Immediately Heidi wanted to know just what he did at school. She had so many questions that even Grandfather began to laugh as Peter tried to answer them as fast as Heidi thought them up.

After Heidi was satisfied, Grandfather made dinner. When Peter was finished, he thanked the old man an invited both of them to come and visit his grannie. Heidi was delighted at the idea of going to visit someone, so the very next morning she asked her grandfather to take her there. But Uncle Alp tried to put her off by saying that the snow was too deep.

But the idea of visiting Grannie was firmly in her head, and day after day she mentioned

Peter Tells Heidi about School.

her wish to visit the old woman to Grandfather. Finally, one morning, Grandfather dragged a big sleigh out of the shed. It had a bar along one side to hold on to and a big steering wheel. They went down the mountain so fast that Heidi felt as though she was flying. She screamed with delight. They stopped with a jerk just outside Peter's hut. Grandfather told her to go in, and he turned up the mountain, pulling the sleigh behind him.

The door Heidi opened led into a small kitchen in which there was a stove and some pots on a shelf. A door led into another small room, which had a low ceiling and was very cramped. In the second room Heidi saw two women. One was mending a jacket and the other one, who was old and bent, sat in a corner. Heidi went straight to the old woman and said:

"Hello, Grannie. Here I am at last."

Grandfather Drags Out a Big Sleigh.

Grannie raised her head and felt for Heidi's hand. Then she said, "Are you the child from Uncle Alp's?" The two women were surprised when Heidi told them that her grandfather had wrapped her up in a warm blanket and brought her down for a visit.

Heidi looked about the room while the women were talking, and she missed nothing.

"One of your shutters is hanging loose, Grannie," she said. "Grandfather will fix it. It will break the window if nothing is done. Look how it bangs to and fro."

"I can't see it, my dear," answered Grannie, "but I can hear it and everything else that cracks and clatters in here. The place is falling apart, and at night I am afraid that sometime it may fall on us and kill us all. And there's no one to do anything about it."

Heidi looked at the old woman.

"Why can't you see the shutter?" she asked. The old woman tried to explain that she

Grannie Feels for Heidi's Hand.

was blind, but Heidi did not understand. She took Grannie's hand and led her to the window so she could look out at the falling snow. The old woman tried again to explain, but Heidi was persistent.

"Even in summer, Grannie? Surely you can see the sunshine and watch it sink behind the mountains and make them all red like fire. Can't you?"

When Grannie sadly shook her head, it was more than Heidi could bear, and she began to cry. She wished she could help Grannie, but there was nothing she or anyone else could do. The old woman tried to comfort the little girl, and she told her that as long as she came to visit, being blind wasn't half so bad. Heidi promised to return very soon and to bring her grandfather along to fix the broken shutter. The women looked at her in disbelief, for the old man hadn't come down to the bottom of the mountain in many years.

The Falling Snow

HEIDI

But after her visit, Uncle Alp was waiting outside to bring Heidi back up the mountain. On the way up, Heidi told him about Grannie and the broken shutter and the little hut that needed so many repairs. The old man did not seem interested in fixing anything for the women, but when Heidi told him how much it meant to her, he agreed.

The very next morning, Heidi and her grandfather appeared at the little hut. Heidi ran in and kissed Peter's mother and Grannie. Soon they heard the sound of a hammer on the outside of the hut. Bridget, Peter's mother, ran outside to see Uncle Alp making all the repairs. She invited him in, but he only said no and kept on hammering.

Uncle Alp Repairs the Hut.

Content in Her Mountain Home

Chapter 5
Two Unexpected Visitors

A winter passed and then another summer, and Heidi's second winter on the mountain was nearly over. She was now seven and had learned many useful things from her grandfather. She visited Peter's mother and Grannie every week and had come to love both women very much. Heidi felt content and peaceful in her mountain home.

Twice during the winter Peter had brought up messages from the schoolmaster in Dorfli to say that Uncle Alp must send Heidi to school. But the old man refused to answer the notes and told Peter that he had no intention of sending Heidi to school.

One March morning, just when the sun began to melt the snow on the slopes, Heidi saw an old man standing outside the hut. He was dressed in black and looked very solemn. He looked at her and said:

"Don't be afraid of me. I'm fond of children. Come and shake hands. You must be Heidi, and where is your grandfather?"

"He's indoors making wooden spoons," she told him and showed him in.

He was the old pastor from Dorfli, who had been a neighbor of Uncle Alp's when he had lived there. He came to tell Uncle Alp that it was time that Heidi went to school. But the old man insisted that Heidi would be better off living on the mountain and learning and growing with the birds and the animals, instead of going off to school where she might learn bad ways. But the pastor insisted that

The Pastor from Dorfli

Uncle Alp return to the village so that Heidi would be able to begin school in the winter. Uncle Alp shook the pastor's hand but said slowly:

"I know what you mean about the child going to school, but I can't do what you ask. That's final. I won't send her to school or come back to the village to live."

The pastor shook his head sadly and walked slowly down the hill. All this left Uncle Alp in a bad mood, and he hardly said a word to Heidi all day.

The next morning, while the old man was still his bad mood, there came a knock at the door. This time it was Detie. She was wearing a hat with a feather and a long dress which swept the ground as she walked. Uncle Alp looked her up and down in silence.

"How well Heidi looks," she said. "I hardly recognize her. Of course I have been meaning to come back for her, but for two years I have

Another Visitor—Detie

been just so busy I haven't had a chance to return!"

Then Detie went on to explain that all the time she had been away she was looking for a proper home for Heidi. Now she had finally found one. There was a rich family who lived in the city. They had a young daughter who was paralyzed and had to spend all her time sitting in a wheelchair. The girl was very lonely, and the family had been looking for a playmate and companion for her. So Detie immediately thought of Heidi and came straightaway to bring her back to the city.

The old man said that he wouldn't part with the child, but that did not stop Detie. She became quite angry with Uncle Alp and told him how she had heard in the village about his refusal to send Heidi to school. She threatened to take him to court if she was stopped from taking Heidi with her. The old man got very angry.

Grandfather Is Very Angry.

"That's enough!" he thundered. "Take her then and spoil her. But don't ever bring her back to me. I don't want to see her with a feather in her hat or hear her talk to me as you have done today." Then he strode away.

Heidi looked very unhappy and went to run after the old man. Detie grabbed her and told her to pack her clothes and prepare to leave. Heidi refused. But Detie told the child that the old man wanted her to leave for the city. When Heidi still refused to go, Detie promised her that she could buy a nice present for Grannie and return to the mountain whenever she wanted to. This sounded better to Heidi, and she daydreamed about surprising Grannie with some soft white rolls from the city.

Heidi Leaves with Detie.

A Fashionable House in the City

Chapter 6
A New Life Begins

The house in the city to which Heidi was being taken belonged to a wealthy man called Mr. Seseman. His only daughter, Clara, was an invalid and spent all her days in a wheelchair. She was a very patient child, with a thin, pale face and mild blue eyes. Her mother had died many years ago, so her father had hired a housekeeper to take care of the little girl. The housekeeper's name was Miss Rottenmeier. She was a capable woman, but she was very strict and never laughed or even smiled. Since Mr. Seseman was so wealthy he also hired two servants, Sebastian and Tinette, to take care of the big house.

When Heidi and Detie arrived at the house, Clara was sitting up in her wheelchair expecting them. They stood in the doorway and waited for Miss Rottenmeier to invite them inside.

Miss Rottenmeier led them into the large sitting room and looked Heidi up and down She did not like what she saw. Heidi was wearing a shabby cotton dress, which was the only kind she had.

"What's your name?" asked Miss Rottenmeier.

When Heidi answered, the housekeeper looked astonished.

"That can't be your *real* name!" she said.

But before Heidi had a chance to answer, Detie interrupted and explained to the woman that Heidi was shy and had never been in the city before and that her real

Clara

name was Adelheid, after her mother. Miss
Rottenmeier continued to question Heidi,
and when she found out that Heidi could
neither read nor write, she became quite
upset. She did not think that this shabby little girl from the mountains would be a fit
companion for Clara. But Detie would hear
none of it and quickly left the house, promis-
ing to return if things did not go well.

All this time Heidi had not moved, not even
when Detie left her. Clara, who had watched
everything from her wheelchair, now called
her over.

"Do you want to be called Heidi or Adelheid?" she asked.

"Everyone calls me Heidi. That's my
name," she answered.

In a short time, Clara and Heidi got to
know each other. Clara explained that her
life was lonely and dull. She had only her
tutor, Mr. Usher, to keep her company. But

Miss Rottenmeier Questions Heidi.

now she had Heidi, and she was looking forward to having a friend. Before Heidi had time to answer and to tell Clara that she would be returning soon to her grandfather, Peter and Grannie, Miss Rottenmeier walked into the room and announced that dinner would be served.

The dining room was the biggest room Heidi had ever seen. Beside Heidi's plate lay a nice white roll, and her eyes lit up at the sight of it. She knew Grannie would love this soft bread. When Sebastian offered her a dish of baked fish, Heidi asked if she could have the roll. Sebastian nodded. When Heidi picked up the roll and put it in her pocket, he could hardly keep a straight face.

Then Heidi tried to talk to Sebastian, and Miss Rottenmeier began a long lecture on table manners and why she should never talk to the servants during dinner. When she was quite through, she turned to Heidi only to

The Biggest Room Heidi Has Ever Seen

discover that the child, who had had a long day, was fast asleep.

Sebastian carried the sleeping Heidi up the winding staircase to a beautiful room. She opened her eyes just long enough to see a bed such as she had never seen before. There were lovely soft sheets and four plump pillows at the head of the bed. As soon as her head touched the pillow, Heidi was asleep again.

Sebastian Carries the Sleeping Heidi.

Heavy Curtains

Chapter 7
A Bad Day for Miss Rottenmeier

Heidi awoke the next morning and looked around her. She forgot where she was and rubbed her eyes a few times until she remembered that she was no longer in the hut with her grandfather.

She jumped out of bed and dressed quickly. She went first to one window, then to the other, and tried to pull back the curtains so that she could see what was outside. The curtains were so heavy that she could only pull them a little bit away from the window. But still, all she could see were walls and windows. She began to feel frightened. At Grandfather's she had always gone out of doors first thing in the morning to see the sky, trees and flowers. Heidi felt trapped in the house, and she could not understand what life in the city could be like.

Just then, there was a tap at the door, and Tinette, one of the servants, announced that breakfast was ready. Heidi really had no idea what breakfast was, since Grandfather had never announced meals in so formal a way. So she got in the bed in her room and waited. After a while Miss Rottenmeier came up and scolded Heidi for being late and led her downstairs to the dining room.

After the meal, Heidi found herself alone with Clara. Soon Heidi was chatting about her life at home with Grandfather and all the things she loved so much on the mountain. While they were talking, Mr. Usher, the tutor, arrived. Miss Rottenmeier took him

Heidi Waits in Her Room.

aside and explained that Heidi was with Clara. She told Mr. Usher that the child could neither read nor write, and that she feared she could never learn. But Mr. Usher was a fair man, and he said he would like to meet the child and see for himself. So Miss Rottenmeier led him into the study, and she went into another room.

Suddenly, there was a tremendous clatter in the study, as though a lot of things had fallen down. Miss Rottenmeier hurried into the room and found the floor strewn with books, paper and ink. Heidi was nowhere to be seen. Mr. Usher explained that Heidi had just rushed across the room, caught the table-cloth as she went by, and swept everything onto the floor with it. Miss Rottenmeier was very angry, and she hurried off to find Heidi. She finally found her standing by the open door, looking up and down the street with a puzzled expression on her face. Heidi thought

Mr. Usher Wants to Judge for Himself.

she had heard the rustling of fir trees, but it had only been the sound of a carriage moving over the cobblestone streets. Miss Rottenmeier was very angry, and she made Heidi promise that she would sit still in her chair during her lessons and never again run from the room. Heidi accepted this as one more rule she had to obey.

After Tinette cleaned up the room, Mr. Usher left and Clara went to take a nap. Heidi did not have anything to do, so she asked Sebastian if he could open one of the big, heavy windows. He helped her up on a stool so she could look outside. But all Heidi could see were buildings and stony streets. She asked Sebastian where she could go to see the whole valley. He answered that she would have to go high up in the church tower to get a view of the entire city.

Heidi climbed down from the stool and ran downstairs and out the front door. But she

Down the Big Stairs

could not seem to find the tower. She walked down many winding streets and passed many people, but they all seemed in such a hurry that she did not dare stop them to ask directions.

Finally she saw a boy standing at a corner. He held a small tambourine in one hand and a large tortoise in the other. Heidi went up to him and asked him how she might find the church tower. He said he would take her there, but that it would cost her a quarter. She thought for a minute and then told him that she hadn't any money, but that Clara did and would be happy to give it to him. So the boy led Heidi through the winding streets.

When they finally reached the church, an old man opened the door for them. Heidi explained that she wanted to see the view from the tower. The old man scratched his head but showed her the way up to the tower

A Boy with a Tambourine and a Tortoise

anyway. But when Heidi looked out, all she could see was a sea of roofs, chimneys and towers. Heidi was so disappointed that the old man decided to try and cheer her up.

"Come and look at our kittens," he said. "Maybe you would like one."

When Heidi saw the furry little creatures she cried with delight. She could hardly believe her ears when she heard the old man say that she could have some of her very own. She chose an all-white kitten and a brown one, and put one in each pocket. Then she said good bye to the old man and told him that there was plenty of room in the big house for the rest of the kittens. He asked her where she lived and promised to bring the rest if he couldn't find homes for them. Then Heidi asked the boy to help her find her way back home.

Soon they reached the house. Heidi pulled the bell and Sebastian came to the door. He

Furry Little Kittens

was very worried and asked Heidi where she had been.

When Heidi went into the dining room, there was an awful silence. Miss Rottenmeier looked very cross and said:

"It was extremely naughty of you to leave the house without asking permission or saying a word to anyone, and then to go roaming about until this late hour. I've never heard of such a thing."

"Meow," came the reply.

"How dare you make fun of me!" shouted Miss Rottenmeier.

But before Heidi could answer, the kittens began meowing again. Miss Rottenmeier got so angry that she stood up and started to shake her finger at Heidi, when the two kittens fell out of Heidi's pockets.

"What! Kittens here?" screamed Miss Rottenmeier. And she rushed out of the room, calling for Sebastian. She called for him to

"What! Kittens Here?"

get rid of the kittens at once.

Sebastian was laughing so hard that he had to wait outside the door to compose himself before he could come in. But now Clara had the kittens on her lap and was delighted with them.

"Sebastian, you must help us," said Clara. "Find a corner where Miss Rottenmeier won't look and hide the kittens there. She will certainly get rid of them if she sees them, but we want to have them to play with when we're alone."

Sebastian smiled and said he had just the place for them. He could tell that with Heidi around there would be even more excitement in the future, and he always enjoyed seeing prissy Miss Rottenmeier in a rage.

Sebastian Laughs Behind the Door.

The Boy Comes for His Quarter.

Chapter 8
Strange Goings-On

The next morning just after Sebastian had opened the door for Mr. Usher, the bell rang again. Sebastian flung the door open and saw the boy with the tambourine who had led Heidi to the church tower.

"What do you want?" he asked.

"I came to see Clara," he said. "She owes me a quarter."

Sebastian accused the boy of lying and said he had no idea what the boy could be talking about. But the boy insisted, and Sebastian soon came to the conclusion that this had something to do with Heidi's adventure the day before. So he showed the boy to the study.

Miss Rottenmeier was in another room when she thought she heard the sound of a tambourine coming from the study. She entered the room and could hardly believe her eyes.

"Stop, stop at once!" she cried when she saw the raggedy boy playing his tambourine for Heidi and Clara. She ran towards the boy, but tripped on something on the floor. Looking down, she saw to her horror a strange, dark object at her feet. It was the tortoise. She leaped in the air to avoid it, then she screamed at the top of her lungs for Sebastian. He was just outside the door, doubled up with laughter. When he came into the room, Miss Rottenmeier had collapsed onto a chair.

"Get rid of that boy and his animal at once!" she ordered.

Miss Rottenmeier Trips on the Tortoise.

HEIDI

Sebastian led the boy to the door and put some coins into his hand to thank him for his music.

In the meantime, Clara, Heidi and Mr. Usher continued their lessons, and Miss Rottenmeier stayed in the study to supervise.

In a little while, Sebastian returned and handed Clara a big basket. He explained that someone had dropped it off at the house and it was for her. Clara opened the lid, and suddenly the room was swarming with kittens. The jumped out one after another and rushed madly about, some biting Mr. Usher's pants, and others climbing up Miss Rottenmeier's skirt. The whole room was in an uproar, and Clara was delighted.

At this point Miss Rottenmeier began to shriek. She called for Sebastian and Tinette to get rid of the animals at once. They came and put the kittens back in the basket and hid them in the attic with the other two.

Swarming with Kittens

HEIDI

Then Miss Rottenmeier turned to Heidi. "Adelheid," she said very sternly, "I can think of only one punishment for such a little savage as you. Perhaps a spell in the dark cellar among the bats and rats will tame you and teach you to behave."

Clara protested loudly. "Please wait till Papa comes home! He will be here very soon, and I'll tell him everything, and he'll decide what is to be done."

Miss Rottenmeier knew that she could not object to what Clara was saying, for Mr. Seseman would be very angry if he heard that Clara had been upset over this matter. So Miss Rottenmeier agreed, but she added that she too would talk with Clara's father when he arrived.

Heidi still could not understand what she had done wrong. But she became very sad and fell asleep dreaming about her home so far away.

Dreams of Her Mountain Home

Mr. Seseman Returns.

Chapter 9
A Bad Report to Mr. Seseman

A few days later Mr. Seseman arrived at the house. The first thing he did when he got inside was to go and find Clara. He hugged his little girl and told her how much he had missed her. Then he turned to Heidi, who was standing beside Clara, and shook her hand.

He asked Heidi if she and Clara got along well. Heidi nodded her head and said that Clara was a good friend. Mr. Seseman smiled and told the girls that he would eat dinner and join them later on.

HEIDI

He went along to the dining room, where Miss Rottenmeier was making sure that everything was in order. When he sat down, the housekeeper lost no time telling him about what had happened in the last few days. She went on to tell him that she thought Heidi was a disgraceful child. But Mr. Seseman knew Miss Rottenmeier quite well and paid little attention to her complaints. Finally, she told him that she did not think that Heidi was right in the head.

Mr. Seseman had not taken her earlier complaints seriously but this was another matter. If it was true, Clara could come to some harm. Since he didn't really trust Miss Rottenmeier's judgment, he decided to talk to Heidi himself.

Mr. Seseman finished his meal quickly and excused himself. He then went into the study to have a talk first with Clara. Since Heidi was there with Clara, he thought for a

Miss Rottenmeier Tells What Has Happened.

moment. It would be difficult to ask Clara about her friend while she was still in the room, so Mr. Seseman asked Heidi to bring him a glass of water.

"Fresh water?" asked Heidi.

"Oh yes—fresh water," he answered.

After Heidi left the room, he pulled his chair closer to his daughter and stroked her hand. Then in a kind voice, he asked Clara to tell him all about the animals, the street musician, and Heidi's strange behavior. Clara explained everything. When she was finished, her father laughed heartily.

"Well, well, then you don't want me to send her home. You're not tired of her?"

"No, no, Papa," she exclaimed, "since Heidi's been here, all sorts of wonderful things have happened. It's really fun having her here. She tells me wonderful stories about her life on the mountain and her grandfather."

Heidi Goes for Water.

HEIDI

Just then, in walked Heidi. She had walked all the way to the village fountain in order to get Mr. Seseman a glass of really fresh water. Heidi told Clara and her father of the kind man she met who asked her who she was and why she was carrying water back to the house. The man had a nice smile, wore a thick gold chain, and carried a walking stick. Clara immediately recognized him as her doctor. Mr. Seseman smiled at the thought of what his old friend would have to say about this unusual search for water to quench his thirst.

That evening he informed Miss Rottenmeier that Heidi was to stay. He said he found her perfectly normal, and he thought she would be a suitable friend for Clara. He also added that she should be treated with kindness at all times. Then he informed everyone that his mother, Clara's grandmother, would be coming to visit after he left on his business trip.

Really Fresh Water!

A Kind Grandmother

Chapter 10
Grandma's Visit

Clara could hardly control her excitement when she learned of her grandmother's visit. She told Heidi all about her and how much fun it would be to have her in the house again.

When the day finally came, even Heidi was excited about Grandma's visit. As soon as Heidi saw the old woman, she loved her at once. She saw the kind expression in her eyes and the way her white hair curled in tiny ringlets about her face. And Grandma liked Heidi too. Despite Miss Rottenmeier's harsh

words, Grandma knew that Heidi was a
bright and loving child.

Not long after Grandma arrived, she discovered that while Clara took her afternoon
nap, Heidi was left with nothing to do. The
child still had not learned to read, and this
concerned Grandma. She could not understand why this was so. She called Heidi
downstairs and asked her to sit next to her
while they looked at picture books. Heidi
was happy to have company in the afternoon
and liked all the lovely pictures Grandma
showed her. But then they came to a picture
of a green meadow with goats and sheep and
a young shepherd, Heidi burst into tears. It
reminded her of the home she loved so much,
and Peter and Grandfather, who were now
so far away.

Grandma dried her tears and decided to
ask her why she had not learned to read.

Heidi confessed that she knew she could

Looking at Picture Books

never learn to read, since Peter had told her how hard he tried but could never learn either. Grandma told her that of course she could learn, and that she must try. She asked Heidi if she would like to read the story that went with the picture of the green meadow and the animals. Heidi thought about it for a minute. How wonderful it would be if she could spend her lonely afternoons reading stories about faraway places!

One morning about a week later, Mr. Usher asked if he could speak with Grandma. He was invited to her room, where he was greeted in the usual friendly way.

"I have something quite remarkable to report," he said. "The impossible has happened. Heidi has learned to read at last. I never thought I would see the day!"

Grandma smiled. That evening she gave Heidi the picture book as a present, and Heidi read the story about the meadow to Clara.

Something Remarkable to Report

A Big Library Filled with Books

Chapter 11
The Joy of Reading

As soon as Heidi learned how to read, she found that life in Mr. Seseman's big house was not so lonely. Now she had friends to keep her company when she was alone in this strange city.

Downstairs in the study there was a big library filled with many books. Some were too long or too difficult for Heidi to read, but there were many she could enjoy. Every afternoon, Grandma would take Heidi aside and ask her if she had finished her last book. If she had, Grandma would take Heidi's hand, and the two of them would go downstairs to the library and choose a new book.

HEIDI

In the evenings, Heidi would take turns reading with Clara and Grandma. Sometimes they would all read a whole book out loud. It made Clara very proud that her friend finally had learned to read, and now they could share the many wonderful things that books had to offer.

But no matter how many books Heidi read, the one Grandma gave her was always her favorite. She read it over and over and kept it in a special place in her room. When she returned to the mountain, she would read it to Grannie.

Mr. Usher now had an easy time with Clara's lessons. Since Heidi had learned to read, the time went much faster, and Clara and Heidi were both eager to learn and full of questions.

Sometimes Mr. Usher would ask Heidi to read a long and difficult passage loud. He

Reading Aloud

was always pleased when she was able to do it easily.

Although the books helped ease Heidi's loneliness, they could not stop her from thinking about Grandfather and her home in the mountains. Every time she looked at her picture book and saw the green meadows and the sheep, her heart longed to return to where she belonged.

Heidi Longs for the Mountains.

A Sad Day for Heidi and Clara

Chapter 12
The House Is Haunted!

Not long after Heidi learned how to read, Grandma announced that she would be leaving. The day of her departure was a sad time for Heidi and Clara. They knew things would not be the same without Grandma. Soon after the old woman left, Heidi began to get very homesick. Every night she cried herself to sleep thinking about her home on the mountain. Sometimes she woke up shaking at the thought that Uncle Alp or Grannie might be sick, or that they would die before she returned. Things got so bad that she grew pale and thin. Even Sebastian looked worried when he saw her pushing her food away.

At about this time, strange things began to happen inside the house. Every morning Sebastian found the front door unlocked and standing wide open. Nothing inside the house was ever missing, so he was sure it wasn't a thief. Some of the servants began to worry.

One evening when Sebastian was up late, he saw a white figure on the stairs. Soon even Miss Rottenmeier was frightened. She wrote Mr. Seseman and asked him to come home at once. But Mr. Seseman did not take her strange story at all seriously. So Miss Rottenmeier told Clara about the open door and the white figure. Clara became so upset that Miss Rottenmeier wrote to Mr. Seseman saying that she feared for Clara's health. This time he believed her and came home at once.

Sure enough, after Mr. Seseman arrived,

Sebastian Finds the Door Open!

he noticed that the front door was unbolted and standing open every morning. He became concerned about this strange occurrence and decided to get to the bottom of things.

The next evening, Mr. Seseman invited his friend, Clara's doctor, to sit up with him and wait for the ghost. The doctor arrived promptly at eight, and the two men sat up talking and drinking strong coffee. Some time after twelve, they heard the distinct sound of a bolt being unlatched. Mr. Seseman exchanged looks with the doctor, and they walked slowly towards the front door.

"Who's there?" asked Mr. Seseman.

The figure turned and gave a little cry. It was Heidi, barefooted and wearing her white nightgown. She began to tremble when she saw the two men.

"Why, Heidi, what are you doing here?" asked the doctor.

"I—I don't know," stammered Heidi.

"Heidi, What Are You Doing Here?"

HEIDI

The doctor took Heidi by the hand and led her away from the door. He talked in a kind voice for a little while. He soon discovered that Heidi had been sleepwalking. She was the ghost that everyone feared so much! After he finished asking her several questions, the doctor realized that Heidi was very homesick—so homesick that her health was beginning to suffer. The sleepwalking was really a symptom of her unhappiness and her longing to escape and return to Grandfather.

The doctor spoke with Mr. Seseman. He explained that Heidi must be allowed to return to the mountain.

"Just look at the child," he said. "She is pale and has lost several pounds in a short time. Without knowing it she has been opening the front door every night. She should be sent home tomorrow. That's my prescription."

Mr. Seseman looked very upset. He knew how much Heidi meant to Clara, but he also

Heidi Was the Ghost!

knew that what the doctor was saying was true. He simply could not be responsible for Heidi becoming ill. He thought for a short time and then turned to his friend and said:

"I know how upset this will make Clara, but I can see how things are. Heidi will leave for her home in the morning."

The Doctor Warns Mr. Seseman.

Miss Rottenmeier Packs Heidi's Trunk.

Chapter 13
Home Again

Mr. Seseman was true to his word, and the very next morning he made arrangements for Heidi's departure. He had Miss Rottenmeier pack her trunk, and he went upstairs to tell Clara the news.

Clara was very distressed by the news, and she tried to make her father change his mind. But she soon saw that he really was right. He promised Clara that he would take her to visit Heidi the following year. This made Clara feel a little better. Then she asked if she could put some nice things in

HEIDI

Heidi's trunk. Mr. Seseman agreed and left Clara to be alone with her plans for gifts for Heidi and her friends at home.

When Heidi found out about the journey, she became so excited she could hardly eat a thing. She was not sure whether she was really awake or just dreaming. But when Sebastian brought down her trunk, she knew everything was real.

Clara packed some warm blankets, dresses, hankies and sewing things for Heidi. Then she showed her the special surprise. It was a big basket of soft white rolls for Grannie. Heidi kissed Clara warmly and held her hand, and the two friends said their good-byes.

Since the trip back to Dorfli was a long one, Sebastian offered to go with Heidi. They took a train from the city and didn't arrive in Dorfli until the next day. Heidi held the basket with the rolls on her lap the whole time. She worried that Grannie might be sick or even

Clara's Special Surprise

dead. But as the train chugged to a stop, she became excited and happy.

When they reached the station, Sebastian asked an old man driving a carriage which was the best way to get to Dorfli. The old man said he would take them there. Sebastian wasn't completely sure that the roads were safe in this country town. But Heidi knew that the roads were passable this time of year and offered to continue the journey on her own. Sebastian loaded her trunk onto the carriage and handed her a fat packet and a letter for her grandfather.

"The packet is for you. It's a present from Mr. Seseman. The letter is for your grandfather. It will explain everything," said Sebastian as he bent down to kiss Heidi good-bye.

The man with the carriage was the baker from Dorfli. He had known Heidi's parents

The Train Arrives in Dorfli.

and realized at once who she was. They chatted a little bit as the horse pulled them up the hill to the village. When they reached Dorfli, the baker lifted Heidi down. She thanked him and told him that Grandfather would pick up the trunk later.

As soon as the carriage pulled away, Heidi rushed uphill as fast as she could go. She had to stop every now and then to catch her breath, for her basket was heavy and the mountain was very steep. But all she could think about was Grannie.

When she reached the hut, she raced up to the door but could hardly open it because she was trembling so much. But she managed it and threw into the little room quite out of breath and unable to say a word.

"Goodness me," someone said from a corner of the room, "that was how Heidi used to come in. How I miss her!"

"It's me—Heidi!" she cried and threw

Heidi Rushes to Grannie.

herself on the old woman's lap and hugged her. She was so happy she could hardly speak. Grannie was so surprised she could not speak either. She stroked Heidi's hair, and a few big tears from her old blind eyes fell onto Heidi's hand.

"It's really you, child," she said.

"Yes, really and truly, Grannie. Don't cry. I'm here and I'll never go away again," said Heidi as she held back her own tears.

Then Heidi handed Grannie the basket and brought out the rolls. One by one she laid them on Grannie's lap.

"Now you won't have to eat hard bread for a while," she said.

Grannie smiled. She could hardly believe all this was really happening. Just then Peter's mother came into the hut. She rushed to Heidi and gave her a big kiss. Heidi talked with the two women for a little while, then said good-bye and began the long climb up

"It's Really You, Heidi!"

the mountain to Grandfather.

The air was cool as Heidi made her way up the steep hill. Everything seemed even more beautiful than she remembered. The peaks of the mountains were snow-covered, the pasture land and the valley below were all red and gold, and there were pink clouds floating in the sky. It was all so lovely that Heidi stood with tears pouring down her cheeks as she breathed in the fragrant air.

Soon, she could see the tops of the fir trees, then the roof, then the whole hut, and then Grandfather himself. He was sitting on the bench outside and smoking his pipe, just as he used to do. Heidi ran towards him and flung her arms around him. For the first time in years his eyes were wet with tears of gladness. He sat Heidi on his knee and looked her over.

"So you've come back, Heidi," he said, "and you don't look so very grand either. Did they

Home Again!

send you away?"

Heidi told Grandfather everything about her life with Clara and how kind they all were to her. Then she told him about her homesickness and the doctor's advice. When she finished, she ran and brought him Mr. Seseman's letter and the packet.

Uncle Alp read the letter and put it in his pocket without saying a word. He told Heidi that the packet contained money for her to use as she wished. Then Heidi and her grandfather sat down and had a big mug of milk and some bread with melted cheese. It was the first time Heidi had had an appetite in a long time.

After a little while, Heidi heard a shrill whistle. She ran out and saw Peter coming down the path surrounded by his lively goats. When he saw her, he stopped dead and stared in astonishment.

As soon as he could get his voice back,

Uncle Alp Reads the Letter.

HEIDI

Peter told Heidi how happy he was to see her again, and the two friends chatted for a while as they watched the sun go down.

When she went inside again, Heidi found that her grandfather had made her a lovely sweet-smelling bed and had covered it with clean linen sheets When she lay down to sleep it was as if she had never been away at all.

Peter Is Happy Heidi Is Home.

Out in the Wonderful Alpine Air

Chapter 14
An Important Day for Grandfather

Heidi stood under the swaying trees, waiting for her grandfather to go down the mountain with her. He was going to fetch her trunk from Dorfli while she visited Grannie. The day was crisp and clear, and Heidi tried to take it all in—the mountains, the fir trees, and the wonderful alpine air.

Soon Grandfather was ready, and they walked down the mountain together. Grannie was overjoyed to see Heidi again, and she told her how much she had enjoyed the soft white rolls from the city. Heidi only wished that she had enough rolls so that Grannie would never have to eat hard bread again. Then she remembered the money that Mr. Seseman had given her. A beaming smile spread over Heidi's face. She would give the money to Peter so that every day he could bring Grannie a fresh white roll from the village. Of course, Grannie protested when she heard this idea. She didn't want Heidi to spend her money on rolls, but when she saw how excited the child was, she agreed.

To entertain the old woman, Heidi reached up on a shelf and brought down a book of hymns. Now that she had learned to read, she could read Grannie her favorite hymns. This made the old woman so happy that she could hardly speak. So for the rest of the day, Heidi chatted with Grannie and read her hymns from the old book.

Soon Grandfather came and tapped on the window to tell Heidi it was time to go home.

Heidi Reads Hymns to Grannie.

HEIDI

On the way back up the mountain, Heidi had so much to tell her grandfather that she talked until they reached the hut. She told Grandfather about her idea for using the money Mr. Seseman had given her. Grandfather smiled when he saw how generous and kind-hearted Heidi was.

That evening at dinner, as Heidi chatted about her life in the city and how kind everyone had been to her, a change came over Grandfather. For the first time in a very long while, he saw the goodness in other people. And he saw this goodness through Heidi's eyes. He realized what a gift this child was, and that his life of bitterness was not good for him and certainly not good for Heidi.

That night Uncle Alp made an important decision. He decided to return to a life that included other people.

The next day was Sunday, and Grandfather told Heidi to get dressed in the clothes Clara

Uncle Alp Makes a Decision.

had given her. Then he took his old blue suit out of the closet. He shined the old brass buttons and even put on a hat. Then together, Grandfather and Heidi walked down the mountain and into the church in the village.

The people of Dorfli were already in church, and the singing had started as Heidi and Uncle Alp went in and sat down in the back. The hymn was hardly over before people were nudging one another and whispering that Uncle Alp was in church. Everyone kept turning around to stare at the old man with the little girl.

When the service was over, Grandfather took Heidi's hand and they went to see the pastor together. They were welcomed into the house by the kind man, and Grandfather first apologized for his behavior so many months ago, when the pastor had come to ask him to send Heidi to school. After a long talk, the two men shook hands, and Uncle Alp agreed

All Dressed Up

to move down to the village during the winter so that Heidi could attend school. As Uncle Alp stood in the doorway shaking the pastor's hand, the people of the village crowded around and offered their best wishes to the old man and Heidi. They could see that something had changed Uncle Alp, and when they heard that he planned to return to Dorfli to live among them, they all wished him well and offered to help with the move.

When at last he and Heidi started for home, many people went part of the way with them, and when they said good-bye, they asked him to visit them in their homes before long. As he watched them go, Heidi saw such a kind light in his eye that she said:

"Grandfather, you look so different—so peaceful. I've never seen you look this way before."

Grandfather smiled and explained that he was happier today than he had been in a very

The Villagers Welcome Uncle Alp.

long time. He had finally given up the bitterness that had made him a lonely old man without friends or neighbors. Now, thanks to Heidi, that was all over. He had begun a new life.

When they reached Peter's cottage, Grandfather went in.

"Good day, Grannie," he said. "I can see I must get busy with some more repairs before the autumn winds begin to blow.

"Goodness me, is it Uncle Alp?" cried the old woman. "What a fine surprise! Now I can thank you in person for all you've done for us."

She held out her hand, which trembled a little, and he shook it heartily. At last the two people Heidi loved most were friends.

Making Friends

The Doctor Is Sad.

Chapter 15
Preparation for a Journey

One sunny September morning, the kind doctor who had been responsible for Heidi being sent home walked along the street to the Seseman's house. It was the sort of day on which everyone should have been happy. But the doctor hung his head in sadness. His hair had grown whiter since the spring, and he wore an air of great sadness. His only daughter had died recently. She had been the great joy of his life since his wife had died some time before. Now he just could not seem to be able to recover his spirits.

Sebastian opened the door and showed him in. Mr. Seseman greeted him in the hall. The two old friends shook hands, and Mr. Seseman could see how unhappy the doctor was.

"I'm glad to see you, doctor. I want to talk to you about the trip to the mountains. Haven't you changed your mind now that Clara seems so much better?"

The doctor became impatient, but he was careful not to lose his temper as he explained to his friend that the long journey to visit Heidi would be more than Clara could take.

Mr. Seseman knew the doctor was right. But he also knew how much this trip meant to his daughter. He just did not have the heart to tell her she would not be able to go.

Then Mr. Seseman had an idea. Why not send the doctor in Clara's place? His friend was looking so poorly that the fresh mountain air and a change of scene would do him a world of good. Besides, he could visit Heidi

The Journey Would Be Too Much for Clara.

and bring back all the news to Clara. When he suggested this to his friend, the doctor thought for a moment, then agreed. Mr. Seseman was pleased with this new plan and hoped Clara would not be too sad.

When she learned that she could not make the trip herself, Clara could not keep the tears from her eyes. But she was told that the trip would only make her health worse, so she blinked back the tears and turned to the doctor.

"Oh please go see Heidi for me. When you come back, you'll be able to tell me all about your trip, and it will be almost as if I'd been there myself."

Then Clara began planning what little presents she would give the doctor to take to Heidi and her friends.

The packing was no easy task, for there were many things that Clara wanted to include. First there was a thick coat with a

Mr. Seseman Tells Clara.

hood, so that Heidi could go and visit Grannie during the winter. Next came a warm shawl for Grannie to wrap herself in when the cold winds howled around the small cottage. Then there was the box of little cakes for her to eat with her coffee and an enormous sausage for Peter's mother to share with Grannie and Peter. There was a pouch of tobacco for Grandfather and a lot of little surprise packets for Heidi.

The packing was soon done, and Clara waited anxiously for the doctor to pick up the trunk and depart for the mountains.

Presents for Heidi

Heidi Runs to the Doctor.

Chapter 16
A Visitor for Heidi

The cool, crisp mountain air brushed against the doctor's cheeks as he made his way up the mountain to Uncle Alp's hut. He had written Heidi that he would be coming, and she was eagerly awaiting him. As he saw the fir trees swaying at the top of the mountain, he thought he saw someone running towards him. Sure enough, in a few minutes he could see Heidi running down the mountain, waving her hands and shouting to him.

As soon as she was close enough, Heidi jumped up and gave the doctor a warm hug.

HEIDI

He had not expected such a reception, and he thanked her for welcoming him to her home. Heidi was full of questions about Clara, Mr. Seseman, Grandma and even Miss Rotten-meier. The doctor could hardly answer her, since she was so excited she didn't give him a chance to catch his breath.

They went towards the hut hand in hand. But even in her excitement, Heidi could sense the sadness in the doctor's eyes. She knew that something must be making him unhappy, and she made up her mind that during his stay she would make him smile again.

When she introduced Grandfather to the doctor, the two men exchanged handshakes and became friends at once. Heidi had told each one so much about the other that they hardly felt like strangers at all.

Then the doctor gave Heidi the presents Clara had sent her. She loved the winter coat and was looking forward to bringing Grannie

Walking to the Hut

the warm shawl the very next day.

The next morning the doctor climbed up to the goat pastures with Heidi. She chatted away all the time about the goats and their strange little ways and the mountain peaks and the flowers. Heidi led the way to her favorite spot, from which she could look down on the distant valley and up to the great mountains where the snow sparkled in the sunlight.

She sat down beside the doctor and asked him if he thought the home as beautiful as she herself did.

"Yes, Heidi, it's very beautiful here," he agreed, "but can a heart forget its sorrow and be happy even here?"

"No one is sad here, not when there is so much beauty and so much love. Stay with us for a little while and you will see," she said.

The doctor was touched by Heidi's words. He surely had nothing to lose. Life in the city

Heidi's Favorite Place

had become unbearable for him since his daughter's death. He decided to give himself a rest here in the mountains and to enjoy Uncle Alp's hospitality.

The weather was fine and sunny all month, and the doctor went up to the hut every morning and from there went off on long walks with Uncle Alp. Together they climbed high where the fir trees were storm-tossed, and higher still to where the hawks nested. Uncle Alp told the doctor many things about the mountains and about his own life. Soon the two men shared a special friendship. The healthy air, good food, and friendly company began to work like Heidi said they would. The twinkle came back into the doctor's eyes, and his cheeks glowed with a healthy pink color.

With the last day of September, the holiday came to an end. On the day before his return to the city, the doctor appeared at the hut

Climbing to Where the Hawks Nest

looking very sad. He was sorry to go, for he had felt at home on the mountain. Uncle Alp was going to miss him too, and Heidi had grown so accustomed to seeing him every day that she could hardly believe those pleasant times were over. But the doctor promised both his friends that he would return very soon.

He thanked them both for making his vacation so wonderful and went on his way. Heidi stood beneath a fir tree and waved until all she could see was a speck in the distance. As he turned for the last time to wave back, the doctor thought to himself:

"This is certainly a wonderful place for sick minds as well as bodies. Life really seems worth living again!"

Waving Good-Bye

Snow to the Windowsills

Chapter 17
Winter in Dorfli

The snow lay so deep on the mountain that winter that Peter's hut was buried in it up to the windowsills. Fresh snow fell almost every night, so on most mornings he had to jump out of the living room window to leave the house. Uncle Alp remembered his promise to the pastor, and as soon as the first snow fell, he took Heidi and the goats down to the village for the rest of the winter.

Near the church in Dorfli, there was a large, rambling, ramshackle place, almost in ruins. Uncle Alp saw the house and knew that with some repairs and hard work it would be a fine home. So he rented it and began to make it livable. He put up some wooden partitions and laid straw on the floor to make winter quarters for the goats in the back of the house. Inside, he repaired the great oak door and patched up the walls and floors. Heidi loved the house, which was much bigger than the small hut on the mountain. She invited Peter over to explore the place with her. Together, they discovered every little nook and cranny until there were no surprises in the new house.

There was much to do in the winter house, and Heidi was starting school. She soon got used to living in the village and going to classes every day. Peter, on the other hand, was hardly ever in school. Heidi noticed his absences, and she also knew that he still had not learned how to read. So one evening when she was visiting Grannie, she took

Uncle Alp Makes the House Livable.

Peter aside.

"I've thought of something," she said.

"What?" Peter asked.

"You must learn to read."

"I have learned," Peter answered.

"I mean properly, so that you can read anything," she insisted.

"Can't be done," Peter said.

"I don't believe that any more," she told him squarely, "and neither does anyone else. Clara's grandma told me it wasn't so and she was right."

Peter looked surprised at Heidi's tone. She seemed so sure of herself. Then she offered to help him learn to read, so that he could surprise Grannie, who was feeling ill. At first Peter was stubborn and refused, but when he saw how much it meant to Heidi and how good it would be for Grannie, he agreed.

At once, Heidi was all smiles. She pulled him over to the table, where a book was all

Heidi Decides to Teach Peter.

ready. It was a rhyming ABC which had come in a big parcel from Clara. Heidi liked it so much that she thought it would be just the thing to teach Peter with. They sat down side by side, bent their heads over the book, and the lesson began. Heidi made Peter go over everything again and again to make sure he knew it all before they went ahead. She knew how difficult it was for him and gave him encouragement every step of the way.

During that winter, Peter came regularly for his lessons and made good progress. The snow became so heavy that Heidi could not go to visit Grannie anymore. She knew the old woman would miss her reading aloud. During this time, Heidi worked extra hard with Peter, who came to the house despite the heavy snows.

One evening he came up from the village and announced to his mother:

Lessons

HEIDI

"I can do it!"

"Do what, Peter?" she asked.

Instead of answering his mother's question, Peter reached up and took Grannie's hymn book off the shelf. In a clear voice, Peter read Grannie her favorite hymn. The two women were speechless. They thought they would never live to see the day that Peter would really learn to read.

The next day Peter went to school, and when the teacher called on him, he read just as well as he had the night before. The teacher was pleased and surprised. He soon learned that Heidi had worked a near miracle with her pupil.

As soon as school was over, the teacher went across to the pastor to tell him the news, and they talked about the good influence that Heidi and her grandfather were having in the village.

Peter Reads Out Loud.

May in the Alps

Chapter 18
More Visitors

The winter passed, and it was May again. The last snows had disappeared, and the little mountain streams raced in full flood down to the valley. The mountainsides were green again and bathed in warm, clear sunlight. The flowers were opening their petals among the fresh green grass.

Heidi was back on the mountain. She listened to the sound of the wind blowing down from the heights, gathering strength as it came nearer. She listened to the hum and buzz of the insects, and everything seemed to be saying, "It's spring, and we're back on the mountain!"

Soon Heidi's quiet pleasure was interrupted by the bleating of Peter's goats. She ran to meet him and he handed her a letter. The postman had given it to him that morning, and he had almost forgotten to come up the mountain and present it to Heidi.

Heidi looked at the letter carefully, then ran to Grandfather. It was a letter from Clara, which she wanted him to read aloud so they could both share it.

Clara wrote that she would be there in a very short time. Her health had improved, and the doctor had told her it would be safe to travel. She would be coming with Grandma. Heidi was so excited she could hardly speak. She was so overjoyed that she felt she must go down to tell Grannie the wonderful news. It was delightful to go running down the mountainside in the bright sunshine

Sharing the Letter

with the wind at her back.

Grannie was in her usual corner, spinning, but she looked sad and worried. Peter had already told her the news, and she was afraid that Clara was coming to take Heidi back to the city with her. Although the old woman would not admit what was really on her mind, Heidi knew her well enough to realize that something was wrong. So Heidi read to Grannie for a long time, and when the old woman saw how happy the child was, the troubled look left her face.

It was dusk when Heidi went home, and the stars came out one by one as she climbed up to the hut. She stopped to gaze up at them, feeling a deep peacefulness inside. She was thankful to be alive and to be here in the place she loved so much.

Gazing at the Stars

A Remarkable Procession

Chapter 19
Clara Arrives

May passed, and June came with longer days and hotter sun, which brought the flowers out all over the mountain. They filled the air with their sweet scents. Heidi came out of the hut looking for some flowers to place on the table when she gave a shout which brought Grandfather running.

"Come and look! Come and look!" she shouted.

When he looked in the direction she was pointing, he saw a remarkable procession coming up the mountain. First came two men, carrying between them a chair on poles, and in it sat a girl, very-carefully wrapped up. A stately-looking woman rode on horseback behind them, gazing about with interest. Then came two more men, one pushing an empty wheelchair and the other carrying an enormous bundle of rugs and wraps in a basket on his back.

Heidi knew at once that Clara had finally arrived. She ran across the grass to welcome her friend. When Heidi reached Clara, the two girls hugged each other and shouted for joy. Heidi turned to Grandma Seseman and gave the old woman a welcoming embrace.

"My dear Uncle Alp," Grandma exclaimed, "what a magnificent place to live! I can't imagine anything more beautiful. And Heidi looks so wonderful. It does me good to see her here where she belongs."

Uncle Alp smiled and welcomed Clara and her grandmother. Then he brought the

Heidi and Clara Hug Each Other.

wheelchair forward and spread some rugs in it. He asked Clara if he could carry her the rest of the way in her usual chair. She consented and they all made their way up to the hut.

Clara could not take her eyes off the scene which stretched before her. She had spent all of her life cooped up inside a house in the city. All this beauty was quite new and remarkable to her.

"Oh, Heidi, if only I could run about with you and look at all the things I know so well from what you have told me!" Clara said.

Heidi took hold of Clara's chair, and pushing with all her might, she managed to get it as far as the fir trees. Both Clara and Grandma stopped and admired the tall, majestic trees. Then Heidi wheeled Clara over to the goat-stall and opened the door wide so that she could have a good look inside.

Under the Fir Trees

HEIDI

Clara could not seem to get enough of all the sights Heidi showed her. She asked her grandmother if she could only stay on a little longer so that she could see the meadows and meet Peter and Grannie. But Grandma Seseman just smiled and told Clara to enjoy what she could and not to think about anything else.

During the tour of inspection, Grandfather had arranged the table and chair and put everything out for their meal. Milk and cheese were warming on the stove, and before long everyone sat down to dinner. Grandma was delighted with the unusual "dining room" with its view of the valley and mountain peaks. Clara ate heartily and exclaimed that nothing in the city had ever tasted so good.

"Just keep it up," said Grandfather. "It's our good mountain air—it more than makes up for our cooking!"

A Hearty Dinner

HEIDI

Grandma and Uncle Alp chatted while the two girls exchanged news of their own. Soon Grandma looked towards the west and said:

"We shall have to go very soon, Clara. The sun is going-down, and the men will be back any moment with the horse and your chair."

Clara's face fell when she realized that she would have to leave so soon. There were still so many things she hadn't seen, and she wanted to spend much more time with Heidi.

Uncle Alp glanced at Clara, then he turned to her grandmother.

"I've been thinking," he began, "and I hope you won't object to the suggestion. Suppose you leave Clara here for a while. I'm sure the mountain air will do her good. You brought so many rugs and blankets with you that we could easily make her a comfortable bed. And I promise to look after her and give her all the attention she needs."

Clara and Heidi were overjoyed at his

Clara Doesn't Want to Leave.

words, and Grandma was beaming as she nodded her head in consent. She knew that being here with Heidi and Uncle Alp would be good medicine for her sickly grand-daugter.

Heidi and Clara at once began making plans, and Uncle Alp and Grandma prepared a bed for Clara next to Heidi's up in the loft.

The loveliest moment of the day came after everyone bid farewell to Grandma. Clara was in the hayloft, looking straight out to the starry sky.

"Oh, Heidi," she said, "it feels as if we were riding in a carriage right to heaven."

Clara lay awake long after Heidi was fast asleep. She looked up at the black sky and watched the stars until she finally fell into a deep, restful sleep.

Clara Looks at the Sky.

Steaming Mugs of Milk for Breakfast

Chapter 20
Clara Begins to Enjoy Life

As the sun rose the next morning, Uncle Alp was outside as usual, quietly watching the mists drift over the mountains and the light clouds grow pink as day broke. Then he went inside to see how his guest was doing.

Clara had just opened her eyes and was gazing with astonishment at the sunbeams dancing on the bed. Uncle Alp asked her if she had had a good night's sleep.

"Oh yes," she replied. "I didn't wake up once during the night."

For breakfast, Uncle Alp served the girls

steaming mugs of milk. At first Clara was a little reluctant to drink goat's milk, since she had never tasted it before, but when she saw Heidi drink with such pleasure, she tried it too. The milk was delicious. It tasted as sweet and spicy as if it had sugar and cinnamon in it.

Clara and Heidi had so many plans that they did not know where to begin. But Heidi thought they should first write to Grandma as they had promised to do every day. So the two girls sat outside in the warm sunshine and wrote letters. Clara's eyes kept straying. It was all so wonderful. The wind had died down, and only a gentle breeze fanned her cheeks and whispered through the trees.

The morning passed in a flash, and Uncle Alp brought them two bowls of milk, saying that Clara should stay out of doors as long as it was light. So they had another hearty meal outside. Afterward, Heidi wheeled

Writing to Grandma

HEIDI

Clara under the shade of the fir trees, where they spent the afternoon telling each other everything that had happened since Heidi left the city.

And so, Heidi and Clara passed two weeks, sitting outside, talking, eating big meals, and enjoying life on the mountain. After a while, Uncle Alp noticed a distinct improvement in Clara's health. She began to look more robust, and she had a rosy glow to her cheeks. So the old man began trying to get Clara on her feet every morning before putting her in her chair. At first, Clara was afraid to stand alone, since it hurt her, but each day she tried a little harder.

Soon Uncle Alp promised the two girls that he would take them up to the pastures.

Uncle Alp Helps Clara to Her Feet.

Uncle Alp Brings Out Clara's Wheelchair.

Chapter 21
The Unexpected Happens

Uncle Alp stood outside the next morning. He looked up at the sky to make sure it would be good weather for the journey up the mountain to the pastures. The girls were looking forward to the trip so much that he hated to disappoint them. But it looked like a fine day, so he brought out Clara's wheelchair and put it in front of the hut before going inside to wake the girls.

After a big breakfast, Heidi, Clara and Grandfather began the trip up the mountain.

When they reached the pasture, they saw

the goats grazing peacefully in little groups and Peter stretched out full length on the ground.

"Now enjoy yourselves," said Uncle Alp, as he prepared to leave them. "Your dinner is in the bag over there in the shade."

There was not a cloud in the deep blue sky. The two girls sat side by side, as happy and contented as could be. From time to time one of the goats came and lay down beside them. After a while, Heidi asked Clara if she would mind waiting while she ran up to the meadow to pick flowers. Clara told Heidi it was fine, and that she would enjoy sitting peacefully and feeding the goats. To Clara, this strange new experience was very exciting. To be here, all by herself, and out of doors in such a beautiful place, with a little goat eating so trustfully out of her hand, was all so delightful. She had never expected to know such happiness and it gave her a new

Sitting and Feeding the Goats

idea of what it must mean to be like other girls, healthy and free. The thought seemed to add something special to the day and to her own happiness.

Suddenly Heidi raced back to Clara.

"Oh, the flowers are so beautiful, you simply must come and see them too. Do you think I can carry you?"

Clara shook her head. She knew that Heidi was too small to carry her, and the chair could never be wheeled up the steep incline. She wanted to walk more than ever now!

Heidi called up to Peter, who came down to the pasture. She told him to hold Clara up on one side, while she took the other. Together they helped her to her feet. So far, so good, but Clara could not keep upright without support.

They tried several different methods, but still, Clara flopped heavily between them. Since Peter was taller than Heidi, Clara was

Peter and Heidi Hold Clara Up.

up on one side and down on the other. She tried putting one foot in front of the other, but she drew it back quickly.

"Try just putting one foot down firmly," said Heidi. "I'm sure it would hurt less."

Clara took Heidi's advice, and sure enough, it really did not hurt half so much.

"Try again," urged Heidi, and Clara did so, taking several more steps.

"Oh, Heidi," she cried, "look at me. I'm walking!"

"Yes you are, you are! All by yourself! Oh, I wish Grandfather was here!"

Clara still kept hold of Heidi and Peter, but with each step they could feel her getting steadier on her feet. Heidi was quite wild with excitement.

"Now we can come up to the pasture every day and wander about wherever we like," Heidi exclaimed, "and you'll never have to be pushed about in a wheelchair again. Oh, isn't

"I Can Walk!"

it wonderful?"

And Clara agreed from the bottom of her heart. Nothing could have been more wonderful to her than to be strong and able to move around like other people.

It was not much farther to Heidi's special spot, where Clara was able to sit down on the warm grass among all the beautiful flowers. She was so affected by all that had happened to her that she was silent as she gazed at all the lovely colors and smelled the delicious scents.

After a while, Clara, Heidi and Peter unpacked the lunch Grandfather had given them. They were all hungry, but Clara and Heidi were really too excited to eat very much.

Not long after they finished their meal, Uncle Alp arrived to take them home. Heidi saw him coming and ran to meet him, eager to be the first one to tell him the amazing

Too Excited to Eat

news. She was so excited that she could
hardly get the words out. But he gathered
what she meant at once, and his face lit up.
He went over to where Clara was sitting and
gave her an understanding smile as he said:

"Something attempted, something won.
This proves you are a strong girl. I am very
proud."

He gave her some support, and she was
able to walk even better than before, but
after a short while, he suggested they rest
and not overdo on the first day.

That evening, Uncle Alp suggested that the
girls write Clara's grandmother. He told
them to invite her for a big surprise.

The next days were the happiest Clara had
ever known. Her waking thought each morning was, "I am well! I can walk!" Each day
she went a little farther alone, and the exercise gave her such an appetite that Uncle Alp
gave her seconds at each meal. This pleased

The Happiest Days of Clara's Life

HEIDI

Uncle Alp, and he took a special pride in Clara's recovery. He felt that the mountain air and all the love he and Heidi felt for the girl had helped her get well.

During that week, Heidi visited Grannie to tell her the good news. As happy as the old woman was for Clara, she herself was not feeling well, and it was hard for her to share in the excitement. Her bed was hard and uncomfortable, but she had to stay there all day. She was too ill to work at her spinning wheel. This made Heidi very unhappy, for she could not help thinking about the wonderful bed she had had at Clara's house in the city. It had many fine, fluffy pillows and a soft mattress. Oh, how she wished she could have that very bed for Grannie!

Grannie Does Not Feel Well.

Heidi Cleans Out the Hut.

Chapter 22
Good-Bye for the Present!

Grandma Seseman received the letter from Clara and Heidi and wondered what the big surprise could possibly be. She wrote back that same day and told them she would be leaving the next morning. Peter brought the letter up in the morning. The girls were already up, waiting for him. As soon as they read the news, they began at once to get everything ready for the big day. Heidi spent the morning cleaning out the hut, while Clara sat and watched her. Then the girls got dressed and sat down outside to wait. Uncle

Alp had been out gathering flowers, and he brought back a big bunch to put inside the hut. Heidi kept getting up to see if there was any sign of their visitor, and at last the little procession came into sight. In front was a guide, leading Grandma's horse, and a man with a laden basket walked behind him. When they reached the little plateau on which the hut stood and the old woman saw the children, she cried out with concern:

"Why Clara, where is your chair? What is this all about?"

But as she came towards them, astonishment took the place of anxiety, and she exclaimed:

"You look so wonderful, my dear. I hardly recognize you."

Then Heidi got up—and so did Clara. Both girls walked slowly towards her. Clara walked with only her hand on Heidi's shoulder for support. Grandma looked on in

The Girls Walk to Grandma.

amazement. They turned and walked towards her, and she saw their two rosy faces were glowing with happiness. Half laughing, half crying, Grandma embraced Clara, then Heidi. She could find no words to express her feelings. Then she saw Uncle Alp, who had come outside and was watching with a pleased smile. She took Clara's arm in hers, and together they went to the old man. Grandma was greatly moved at having her granddaughter walk beside her at last. She grasped Uncle Alp's hand and said:

"My dear Uncle, how can we ever thank you! It is your care and nursing that have done this."

"And love and sun and nature," he added.

"And don't forget the lovely goat's milk," put in Clara.

"Your rosy cheeks tell me that," answered her grandmother. "I really find this all so hard to believe. I can't take my eyes off you.

Grandma Cannot Thank Uncle Alp Enough.

It's a miracle. I must telegraph at once to your father and tell him to come here immediately. I won't tell him why. This will be the greatest surprise of his life."

The little party sat down to dinner in front of the hut, and Grandma was told the whole story right from the beginning.

"I still can't believe it!" she kept saying. "This is all just too good to be true."

As it happened, Mr. Seseman also had been planning a surprise. He had finished his business earlier than he expected and missed Clara so much that he had jumped on a train to Dorfli.

After he reached the little village, he set out on foot to Uncle Alp's hut. He was not used to much exercise, and the long climb up the hill was quite exhausting for him. After a long while, he had not even come to Grannie's hut, so he began to think he must have taken the wrong path. He looked about

A Long Climb

anxiously for someone to ask, but there was not a soul in sight, nor a sound to be heard except the humming of insects and the occasional twittering of a bird.

Mr. Seseman grew very hot, and as he stopped to fan himself, Peter came running down the path, but he was in too much of a hurry even to stop and notice the weary traveler. So Mr. Seseman trudged on. He soon reached Grannie's cottage, so he knew that he was on the right path. He went on from there with more energy, and it was not long before he saw the hut with the three fir trees a little way above him. The sight spurred him on, and he stepped out briskly, chuckling to himself at the surprise he hoped to give everyone up at the hut.

As he stepped thankfully toward the level ground on which the hut stood, he saw two people coming towards him, a tall fair girl, leaning on a smaller girl.

Too Busy Running

He stood still and stared. Suddenly his eyes filled with tears. He was strangely reminded of Clara's mother, who had had just such fair hair and delicate white cheeks. He hardly knew whether he was awake or whether he was dreaming.

"Don't you know me, Papa?" Clara asked. "Am I so different? Am I changed?"

At that, he strode towards her and took her in his arms.

"Changed, indeed!" he cried. "Is it possible? Can I believe my eyes?"

He stepped back a few feet to see her better, then drew her close again. His mother joined them, anxious not to miss a single second of this great moment.

"Well, what do you think of that, my son?" she asked, and then she added, "You thought you'd give us a surprise, a lovely one, but as it turns out, it is nothing to the one we were preparing for you, is it now?" She kissed him

"Can I Believe My Eyes?"

warmly as she spoke.

"Now come and meet Uncle Alp. We owe him so much. I believe both he and Heidi were responsible for all this."

Then Mr. Seseman looked down and gave her a big kiss and a hug.

"I am so glad to see you looking well again too. Why, you look as happy and healthy as you did when you first came to stay with us in the city."

Heidi smiled up at him. She was so pleased that it should be here on the mountain that her good friend had found such happiness.

Then Mr. Seseman and Uncle Alp sat down on the small bench outside the hut. The two men had much to talk about. After Mr. Seseman thanked Uncle Alp again and again, he asked him to tell the whole story of Clara's remarkable recovery. He put out his hand and grasped Uncle Alp's large rough one warmly.

"Dear friend," he said, "I am sure that you

Mr. Seseman and Uncle Alp

HEIDI

will understand what I mean when I say that
for years I have never known real happiness.
What were all my money and my success
worth, if they could not make my poor little
girl well? Money can only buy things, but it
can never bring health or true happiness.
Now you and Heidi have given us both something to live for. That can never be repaid.
But you must tell me if there is any way I
can show my thanks. I will do anything that
is in my power to show my gratitude."

Uncle Alp listened quietly, then he replied:

"I have a share, too, in your joy at Clara's
recovery. In that lies my reward. There is
only one thing I really wish. I am old, and I
cannot expect to live much longer. I shall
have nothing to leave Heidi when I die. She
has no one but me. If you would promise me
that Heidi need never have to go and earn
her living among strangers—that would be
reward enough for me."

Uncle Alp Has Only One Wish.

"That is something you need not even ask," Mr. Seseman answered. "Heidi is already like one of my family. We shall never allow her to be left with strangers. I promise you that. I will make provisions for her during my life and afterwards as well."

"Amen to that," added Grandma, who had stood beside her son during this last part of the conversation.

Then she put her arm around Heidi and asked:

"Have you a wish to be granted?"

"Yes, I have," Heidi replied.

"I am glad. Tell me what it is," answered Grandma.

"The bed I had in the city, with its three pillows and the warm quilt. I would like to have it for Grannie. It would make her so much more comfortable."

"Of course," answered Grandma. "I will telegraph to the city at once and have it sent

Grandma Agrees to Heidi's Wish.

to Grannie's hut in a day or two."

Heidi was so delighted she wanted to run and tell Grannie the good news at once. But Uncle Alp suggested that they all go down and visit the old woman, whom they had really neglected during all the excitement.

Peter saw everyone coming as he looked out the window.

"Oh, dear," sighed Grannie when he told her what he saw, "are they taking Heidi with them back to the city?"

Just then Heidi burst into the hut.

"Grannie, Grannie,'? she cried, "what do you think? My bed from the city is going to be brought here for you."

She expected to see Grannie's face light up at this news, but instead she saw only a sad little smile.

"Oh Heidi, I think I shall die without you," burst out Grannie.

"What's this?" interrupted Grandma Sese-

Peter Sees Everyone Coming.

man. "Heidi is going to stay here with you and Uncle Alp. We shall want to see her too, but we shall come here to visit."

At that, Grannie's face lit up, and she pressed the woman's hand. Heidi hugged her again .

"I did not know there were such good people in the world. It renews my faith in humankind," said Grannie.

Then everyone stood in the hut and shared a very special moment of happiness, love and friendship that none of them would ever forget.

A Special Moment of Happiness